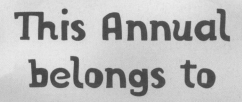

This Annual belongs to

....

the Knight!

EGMONT
We bring stories to life

First published in Great Britain 2013 by Egmont UK Limited
The Yellow Building, 1 Nicholas Road, London W11 4AN

Written by Stephanie Milton.
Designed by Claire Yeo and Cassie Benjamin.

ISBN 978 1 4052 6761 8
54724/1
Printed in Italy

HiT
entertainment

Adult supervision is recommended when glue, paint, scissors and
other sharp points are in use.

Stay safe online. Any website addresses listed in this book are correct
at the time of going to print. However, Egmont is not responsible for
content hosted by third parties. Please be aware that online content
can be subject to change and websites can contain content that is
unsuitable for children. We advise that all children are supervised

 ontents

 ## All answers on page 66.

Good Morrow, Fair Friends!

Young Mike is a knight – the bravest in town!
He's lucky to have the best friends around.

They help him learn how to be a brave knight,
With them by his side, he can do it right!

So step right this way to join in the fun,
Read tales and play games until we're all done!

Sheep Count!
There are ten sheep trotting through the pages of this Annual. Can you spot them all?

A CHANCE TO WIN £150 OF BOOK TOKENS!

See page 67 for details.

NATIONAL BOOK tokens

Mike the Knight

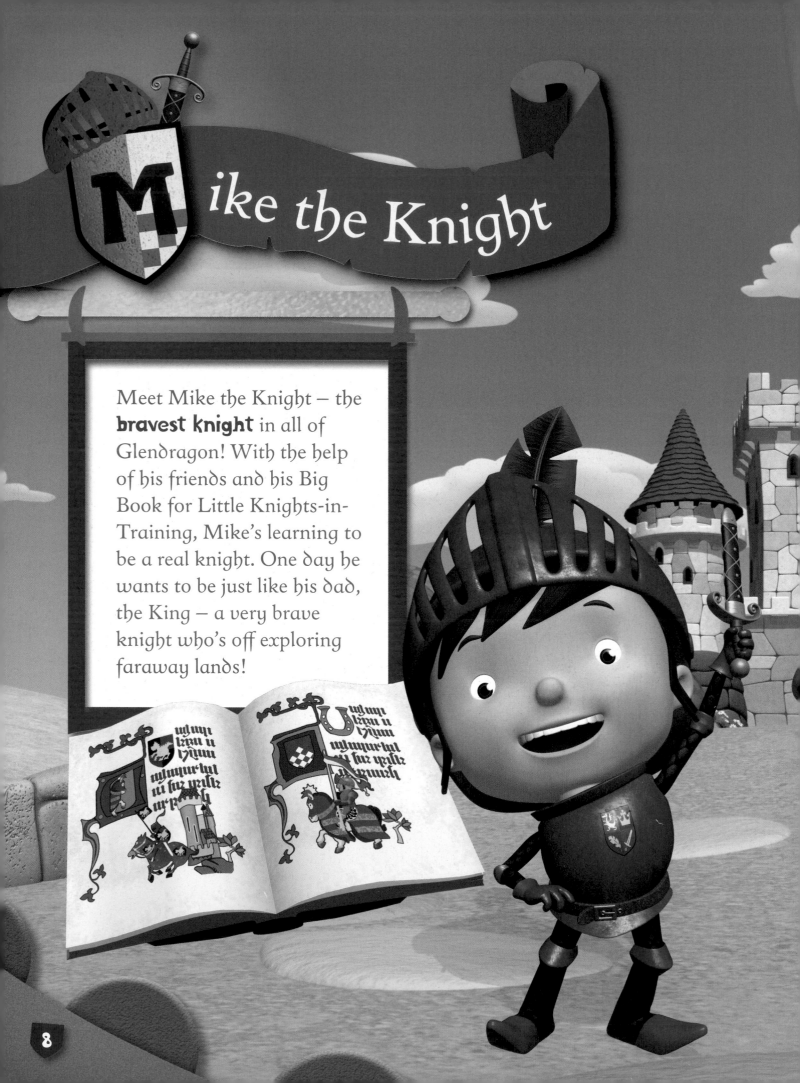

Meet Mike the Knight – the **bravest knight** in all of Glendragon! With the help of his friends and his Big Book for Little Knights-in-Training, Mike's learning to be a real knight. One day he wants to be just like his dad, the King – a very brave knight who's off exploring faraway lands!

Galahad

Galahad is Mike's trusty horse. He's one of Mike's best friends and goes with Mike on all his missions, although he'd rather be back at his stable admiring himself in the mirror. He's very handsome, and loves to be groomed. He also loves showing off his trophies!

Spot the Difference

These two pictures of Mike and his friends look the same, but there are 6 differences. Can you spot them all? Colour in a shield for each one you find.

2

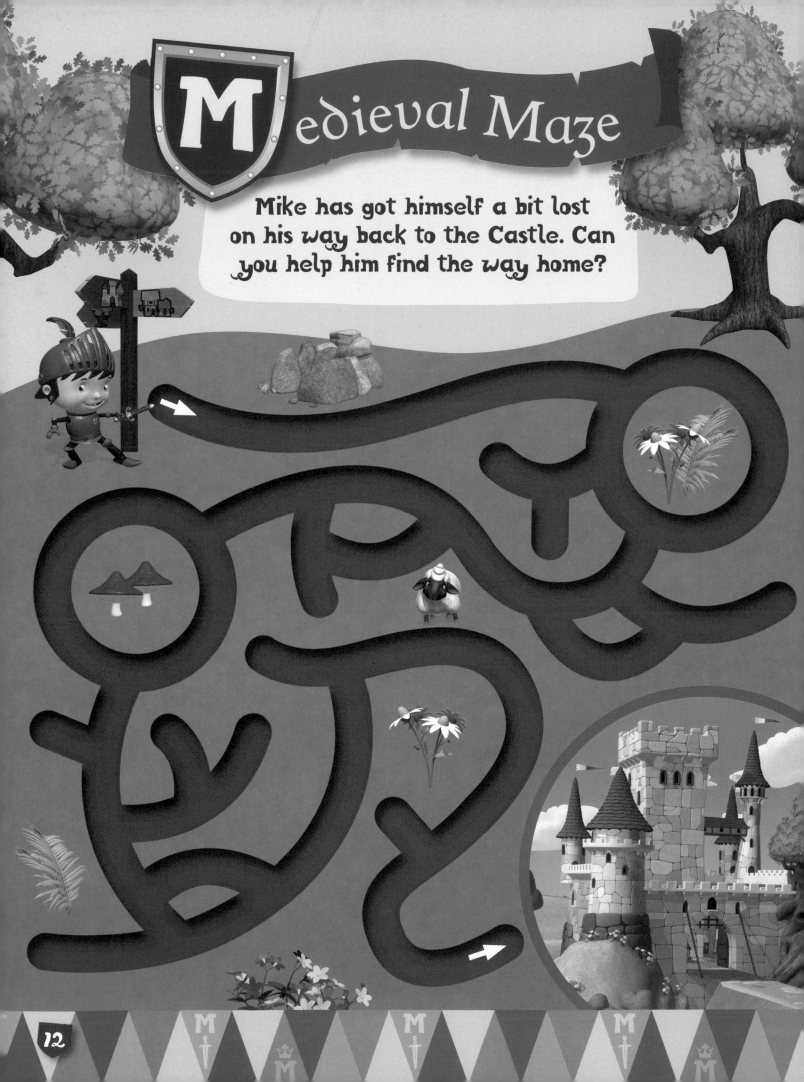

Medieval Maze

Mike has got himself a bit lost on his way back to the Castle. Can you help him find the way home?

Starting at number 1, join the dots to finish this picture of Grey Beard the Viking, then colour it in.

Odd Mike Out

One of these pictures of Mike is different from the rest. Can you put a circle around the odd one out?

Evie's Magical Wordsearch

There are lots of magical things in Evie's workshop. Can you find these magical words in the grid?

Words:
POTION
WAND
SPELL
WIZARD
EVIE
FROG

O	E	J	U	F	G	Q	T	W
R	A	N	S	R	H	V	Y	A
P	O	T	I	O	N	R	D	N
T	Y	A	S	G	A	X	W	D
I	G	D	I	X	E	V	I	E
T	K	S	B	R	K	L	Z	S
A	X	M	E	G	S	I	A	C
W	C	Z	R	P	T	E	R	Q
U	S	P	E	L	L	F	D	A

Sparkie

Sparkie is one of Mike's best dragon pals. He's a big fire-breathing dragon who loves his food and sometimes sets things on fire by accident. He's always ready for fun and a new adventure, as long as he makes it home in time for dinner!

Squirt

Squirt is a small blue dragon who can squirt water out of his mouth. This comes in very handy when his friend Sparkie accidentally starts a fire! He can get scared more easily than Sparkie, but he's just as important to Mike. And being small is a good thing for Squirt, because it means he can fly!

Knightly Campout

Once **upon a time**, in the Kingdom of Glendragon, Mike the Knight was reading about knightly adventures in his Big Book for Little Knights-in-Training. "I want to go on a **knightly adventure**!" Mike told Sparkie and Squirt. Sparkie and Squirt just wanted to have a nap.

Mike looked at a picture of a knight camping in his book. "Maybe there is something knightly about sleeping!" He read aloud: "An important part of a knight's training is to camp out overnight in some **wild woods**!"

Mike jumped up.
"By the King's crown,
that's it! I'm Mike
the Knight, and my
mission is ... to camp
overnight in the Tall
Tree Woods!"

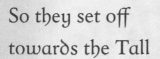

So they set off
towards the Tall
Tree Woods. Mike pulled out his sword. Thanks to one
of Evie's wonky spells it turned into strange objects that
Mike would find useful on his missions. Today it had
turned into a goblet filled with yummy **hot chocolate**!

Mike galloped bravely ahead of Sparkie and Squirt into the woods. He found some branches and tried to make a tent, but they just fell to the floor.

Sparkie and Squirt arrived, puffing and panting and carrying two **enormous** sacks. They had a tent, food, pots and pans, and even teddy bears! Mike looked longingly at Sir Teddy, his favourite cuddly toy. Squirt held Sir Teddy out to Mike.

"No thanks, Squirt. I'm doing this camping mission the **knightly** way, remember? Why don't you make **your** camp, with all **your** things, over there."

Mike went back to making his stick tent. "Would you like some string, Mike?" Sparkie asked. "No thanks! I'm doing this the **knightly** way!" Mike insisted. Galahad snorted. He didn't fancy sleeping out in the cold.

Sparkie and Squirt put up their enormous tent with a spot of magic. It looked **very cosy**.

Mike finished his wobbly stick tent and started to make a bed. He tried not to look at Sparkie and Squirt's comfy mattress.

Once Mike's stick bed was finished, he bounced on it to check how comfy it was.

CRRRACK!

The twigs snapped underneath him.

Sparkie pulled Mike's Big Book For Little Knights-in-Training out of Galahad's saddlebag and turned to the knightly camping page.

"Er, Mike?" Sparkie called. "Are you **sure** you should be camping with almost nothing? **This** knight has a tent, and a comfy camp bed!"

"I want to be even **more knightly** than him!" Mike said. "My bed just needs a few more leafy bits ..."

Sparkie and Squirt started to cook Campout Stew. The delicious smell made Mike realise how hungry he was.

Squirt offered Mike a bowl of stew, but Mike wanted to find his own dinner. Mike could see some apples on a nearby tree, but he wasn't quite tall enough to reach them.

Squirt offered Mike a box to stand on. "Knights don't need boxes!" Mike said crossly. He stood on a strange lump of earth under the tree. But it wasn't just a strange lump of earth ... it was an anthill!

All of a sudden, Mike was covered in ants! He **jumped about**, trying to shake them off. He knocked his stick tent over with a **crash**.

Mike was fed up. Being knightly was **very hard**. Sparkie and Squirt had an idea. "Maybe you could help **us**," Sparkie said, "by tasting our stew to make sure it's **knightly** enough?"

Mike tasted the stew. It was **delicious**! But then he stopped. "My mission is ruined," he said sadly.

Sparkie pulled out the Big Book for Little Knights-in-Training and showed Mike all the things the other knight had. "I can still finish my mission, as long as I camp out all night!" Mike decided. He drew his sword, which was still a goblet of hot chocolate. **"It's time to be a knight and do it right!"**

Sparkie lit a lantern for Mike with his fiery breath, and Squirt gave Mike some string to tie his sticks together. Then Squirt gave him a spare blanket and pillow, and Sparkie gave him a nice big bowl of **Campout Stew**.

Mike realised that the best way
to finish his mission was for
everybody to help each other. He
shared the hot chocolate with his
friends before they went to bed.
They all slept very well.

The next morning, Mike rode proudly back to the Castle.
"A whole night in the Tall Tree Woods, Mike! Well done!
How did you manage?" Queen Martha asked. Mike
smiled. "It was **easy** for a brave knight like me, Mum! I
just needed my horse, some string,
a few other bits and pieces ...
and my **dragon friends**!"

T he End

Bug Swarm

How many Dragon Bugs can you spot?
Count them all, then write the
number in the box.
Can you spy Bird, too?

There are  Dragon Bugs.

Viking Match

Draw lines to match the merry, mischievous Vikings to their shadows.

Copy the Colours

Colour in Sparkie below using the picture opposite as a guide. What do you think Sparkie is up to today?

Look and Find

30

The Castle Treasure Room is filled with shiny things.
Help Mike to find each one in the picture
and tick them off as you spot them.

Evie

Evie is Mike's little sister, and a wizard-in-training! She's always trying out new spells, and sometimes they don't quite turn out how she'd like. But with Mike's help she can always make things right again!

Queen Martha

Queen Martha is in charge of Glendragon while the King is away. She's also Mike and Evie's mum, so she's very busy! Luckily Mike's always around to help when there's a problem to solve. Queen Martha has two dogs, Yip and Yap, who keep her even busier than Mike and Evie!

Mrs Piecrust is famous for baking delicious pies! What do you think her brand new pie looks like? Draw it below, then colour it in.

Look Closely

Mike and his friends love to visit Glendragon Village. Which of the close-ups below can't be found in the big picture?

a

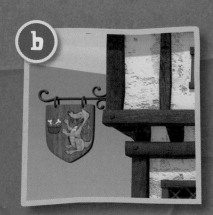

b

c

Dragon Squires

You can help read this story. Listen to the words, and when you come to a picture, say the name.

| Mike | Sparkie | Squirt | Yip | Yap |

**I**t was almost time for the Glendragon parade, and

and Evie were very excited! They were going to ride through the

town, carrying the royal flag.  was grooming

Galahad and Evie was polishing her scooter.

Just then, a postcard arrived from their dad, the King.

It was a picture of the King on his horse, carrying the royal flag,

with his squires by his side. He looked very knightly.

"What are squires?" asked   .

explained that squires were special helpers. This gave

a great idea.

"We could be your squires,   !"   said.

liked the sound of this. For his next mission Mike would

train them to be his squires in time for the Glendragon parade!

 was about to start training his squires when the Queen

arrived and asked him to look after and  while

she got ready for the parade. "Make sure they don't get dirty!"

she said.

 didn't really have time to look after and  .

He gave them a ball to play with and went back to his Very

Important Squire Training.  made  and

practise walking slowly, like humans, instead of galloping and

flying and stomping like dragons. Soon,  had forgotten all

about and .

Meanwhile, and had run off after their

ball and made themselves very dirty!  suddenly realised

that they had gone missing. He had to find them and get them back

to the Castle to clean them up for the parade, fast! Perhaps

and  could help! But they'd have to run really fast,

and fly, like dragons!

 drew his sword — it was a dog bone! With Sparkie and

Squirt's help,  used his sword to lead

and 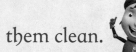 back to the Castle Courtyard. Once and the

dogs were over the drawbridge,  and  raised the

gate so that they couldn't escape again. Now they just had to get

them clean.  had another brilliant idea —  could

fill a tub with water and  could heat it up to make a bath!

Everybody made it to the parade looking clean and tidy, and

  had learned to appreciate  and for

what they were – dragons!

HUZZAH!

The End

Count the Trophies

Galahad has lots of trophies. How many can you see on this page? Count them all, then write the number in the box at the bottom.

There are ☐ trophies.

Colour the Queen

Queen Martha is getting ready for a Royal Banquet. Colour in this picture as neatly as you can.

Pick Your Pie

All of Mrs Piecrust's pies are delicious, so it's hard to choose just one! Follow the lines with your finger to see who gets which pie.

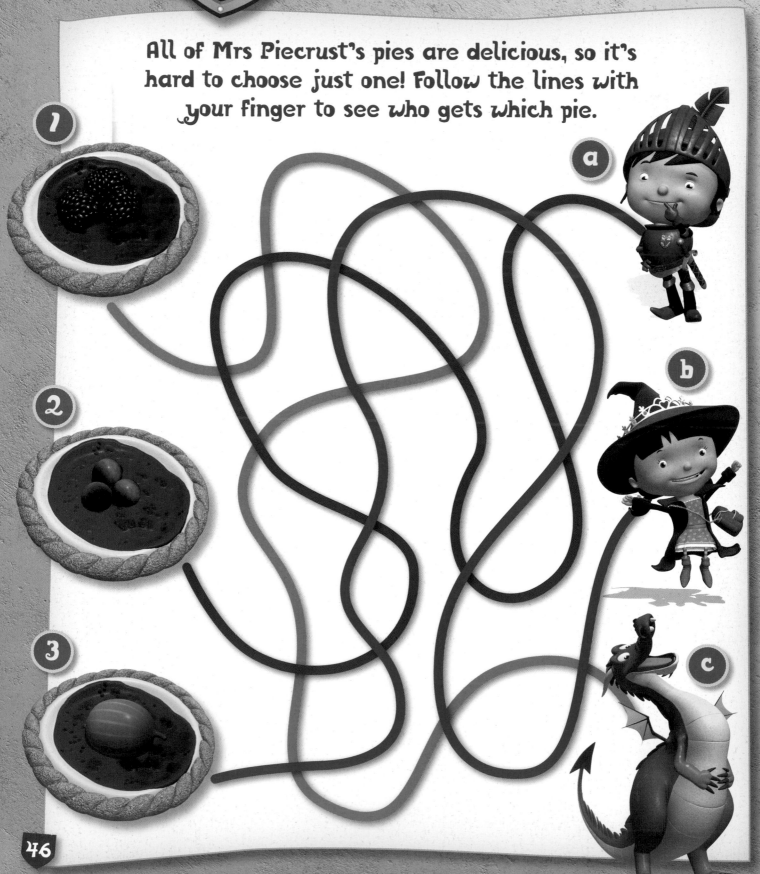

D o It Right!

There are three things wrong with this picture of Mike, Evie and Queen Martha. Colour in a shield each time you spot one.

Trollee

Trollee is a kind little Troll who is best friends with Mike. He'd love to be a knight just like Mike, but he'll settle for going along on missions with him instead! He lives in the Maze Caves with Ma and Pa Troll.

The Vikings

The Vikings come from a far-off land and like to visit Glendragon to cause mischief. Grey Beard, Broken Horn and No Beard like to take things that don't belong to them, and it's up to Mike to put things right and send the Vikings home.

Let's Celebrate!

When Mike's missions go well, there's a special word that Mike and his friends like to shout. Draw over the dotted lines to reveal the special word.

Huzzah!

Maze Cave Shadows

It's dark down in the Maze Caves! Draw lines to match the friendly Trolls to their shadows.

a

1

2

b

c

3

51

Arrow Hunt

Mike has been practising his archery. There are six arrows like this one in Mike's bedroom. Can you spot them all?

Sparkie

Squirt

54

 **D**ot-to-Dot

Starting at number **1**, join the **dots** to finish this picture of Squirt, then colour him in.

Mission Home

One day, Mike and his friends were playing a game of 'Find Your Shield'. Mike had to find his shield whilst wearing a blindfold.

"He's going to find it in no time!" Squirt giggled as he watched Mike stumble into the stable.

A moment later Mike came out, holding the shield.

"You really know your way around, just like your dad!" smiled the Queen as Mike took off the blindfold.

"He went all the way to the **end of Glendragon** once, planted his flag and found his way back without getting lost!" That sounded very exciting to Mike.

"I want to go there too!" he decided.

"I'm Mike the Knight, and my mission is to go to the end of the Kingdom and come back home, without getting lost!"

Mike pulled out his sword, which had turned into a trumpet. He had no idea how that might help him with his mission!

Mike, Galahad, Sparkie and Squirt set off to find the end of the Kingdom. But they weren't sure how to get there! They came to a signpost which showed the way to the Tall Tree Woods, the Village and the Castle. Sparkie and Squirt smiled — at least they'd be able to find their way home again!

"Let's take the sign down," Mike said. "I won't need signs to find my way back!"

Sparkie and Squirt looked worried. "Don't worry," laughed Mike, "we'll put it back when I've finished. Just hide it behind that bush for now."

A little further down the path they met some villagers. The villagers were pushing a cart stacked with yummy food. "We're taking it to the Castle," they explained. "Where are **you** off to, Mike?"

"To the end of the Kingdom!" Mike said. They said goodbye and the villagers went on their way. But when they reached the place where the signpost should be, there was nothing there. How were they going to find the Castle?

Evie and the Queen had been out picking flowers, but without the signpost, they couldn't find their way back to the Castle, either!

Meanwhile, Mike and his friends had reached another sign. Squirt sat

on top of it for a quick rest, and it broke with a crack!
"Now we won't know how
to get home!" Squirt wailed.

Then they saw Ma and Pa
Troll, who were on their way
home for some turnip stew.
They offered some to Mike.
"No thanks!" said Mike. "I'm finding my way to the end
of the Kingdom!" The Trolls set off for the Maze Caves,
but without the signpost, they had no idea which way to
go. They sang a little rhyme to help them choose a path.
But it was the wrong path!

Sparkie and Squirt found a
very old sign carved into a rock
at the side of the strange path.
They could use the sign to find
the way home! But they'd have
to hide it from Mike.

Finally, they reached the end of
the strange path. Right in
front of them, planted in the
ground, was a **royal flag**.

Mike gasped. "It must be Dad's! We made it to the end of the Kingdom!"

"Now we can go home!" Squirt cheered. "And I know the way!" Squirt led them back up the path, and tried to peek at the sign on the rock without Mike seeing. But Mike did see! He came over for a closer look. Squirt leaned against the stone, trying to look casual.

All of a sudden the stone began to roll away. Squirt found himself running on top of the rolling stone, trying to keep his balance!

The stone was heading straight for a group of villagers! Sparkie could see Evie and Queen Martha, too. He was going to crash into them!

Evie pulled out her wand and began to chant.
"Magic, quick, don't make a fuss, stop this stone from hitting us!"

But the stone didn't stop. Instead, Evie and Queen Martha shot up into the air like rockets, dropping their flowers all over the path!

Mike and Sparkie arrived just in time – they caught Evie and the Queen as they fell back to the ground. Everybody laughed with relief!

"We're completely lost!" they told Mike. "Something's happened to the signs!" In a small voice, Mike explained that he had taken the signs down for his mission.

"But the signs are for everyone, and I was only thinking about myself," he realised.

He felt terrible. But then he had an idea.

"It's time to be a knight and do it right! I'll get you home, and put the signs back, too!" Sparkie and Squirt heaved the stone back into place so they could see which way the Castle was.

They could see more lost villagers further down the path. Mike pulled out his trumpet and blew loudly.

"Anyone who's lost will hear the trumpet," he explained, "and they'll follow me home!"

Mike led everybody back towards the Castle. One by one they found the missing signposts and put them back in their proper places so they could see the right path back to the Castle.

Soon, Mike had led everybody safely back to the Castle Courtyard.

"You did it, Mike! You got us back!" Sparkie cheered.

"I couldn't have done it without your help with the signs, Sparkie!" Mike said.
"Well done Squirt, **and** Sparkie, **and** Mike!" the Queen smiled.

They headed into the Throne Room, where they found Ma and Pa Troll sitting in the royal thrones!
"We couldn't find the Maze Caves," Pa Troll explained. Everybody laughed.
"We'll get you home," promised Mike. "But first, why don't you stay for lunch?" So they all sat down to share the **delicious turnip stew.**

The End

Race to the Castle!

Start →

2

3

15

16 Find a shortcut. Move forward a space.

17

18

Take the wrong path. Move back a space.

19

How to play:

- Place the counters on the Start square.

- Take it in turns to roll the dice, moving your counter around the board.

- The first player to reach the Finish wins!

Mike and Galahad are racing Sparkie home to the Castle! Find a friend, a dice and two counters and see who reaches the finish line first.

4 Trip over a rock. Move back a space.

5

6

7 Stop for a rest. Miss a turn.

8

9 Evie gives you a hand. Take another turn.

14

13 Cheered on by your friends. Take another turn.

12 Boulder blocking your path. Miss a turn.

11

10

22

21

23

20

Finish →

nswers

Page 10-11:

Page 12:

Page 14: Picture 5 is different.

Page 15:

Page 26: There are 18 Dragon Bugs.

Page 27: 1—c, 2—a, 3—b.

Page 30-31:

Page 37: Close-up b can't be found in the big picture.

Page 44: There are 19 trophies.

Sheep Count: The sheep are on pages 9, 12, 16, 27, 34, 39, 47, 48, 52 and 65.

Page 46: 1—c, 2—a, 3—b.

Page 47:

Page 51: a—3, b—1, c—2.

Page 52:

Reader Survey

We'd love to know what you think about your Mike the Knight Annual. Ask a grown-up to help you fill in this form and post it to the address at the end by 28th February 2014, or you can fill in the survey online at:

www.egmont.co.uk/mikeknightsurvey2014

One lucky reader will win £150 of book tokens!
Five runners up will win a £25 book token each.

NATIONAL
BOOK
tokens

1. Who bought this annual?

- ☐ Me
- ☐ Parent/guardian
- ☐ Grandparent
- ☐ Other (please specify)

_____

2. Why did they buy it?

- ☐ Christmas present
- ☐ Birthday present
- ☐ I'm a collector
- ☐ Other (please specify)

_____

3. What are your favourite parts of the Mike the Knight Annual?

Stories	☐ Really like	☐ Like	☐ Don't like
Puzzles	☐ Really like	☐ Like	☐ Don't like
Colouring	☐ Really like	☐ Like	☐ Don't like
Character profiles	☐ Really like	☐ Like	☐ Don't like
Posters	☐ Really like	☐ Like	☐ Don't like

4. Do you think the stories are too long, too short or about right?

- ☐ Too long
- ☐ Too short
- ☐ About right

5. Do you think the activities are too hard, too easy or about right?

- ☐ Too hard
- ☐ Too easy
- ☐ About right

6. Apart from Mike, who are your favourite characters?

1 _____

2 _____

3 _____

7. Which other annuals do you like?

1 _____

2 _____

3 _____

8. What is your favourite...

1 ... app or website? _____

2 ... console game? _____

3 ... magazine? _____

4 ... book? _____

9. What are your favourite TV programmes?

1 _____

2 _____

3 _____

10. Would you like to get the Mike the Knight Annual again next year?

☐ Yes

☐ No

Why? _____

Thank you!

Child's name: _____ Age _____ Boy / Girl

Parent/guardian name: _____

Parent/guardian signature : _____

Parent/guardian email address: _____

Daytime telephone number: _____

☐ Please send me the Egmont Monthly Catch-Up Newsletter.

Please post to: Mike the Knight Annual Reader Survey, Egmont UK Limited, The Yellow Building, 1 Nicholas Road, London W11 4AN

GOOD LUCK!

EXCITING CHILDREN'S MAGAZINE

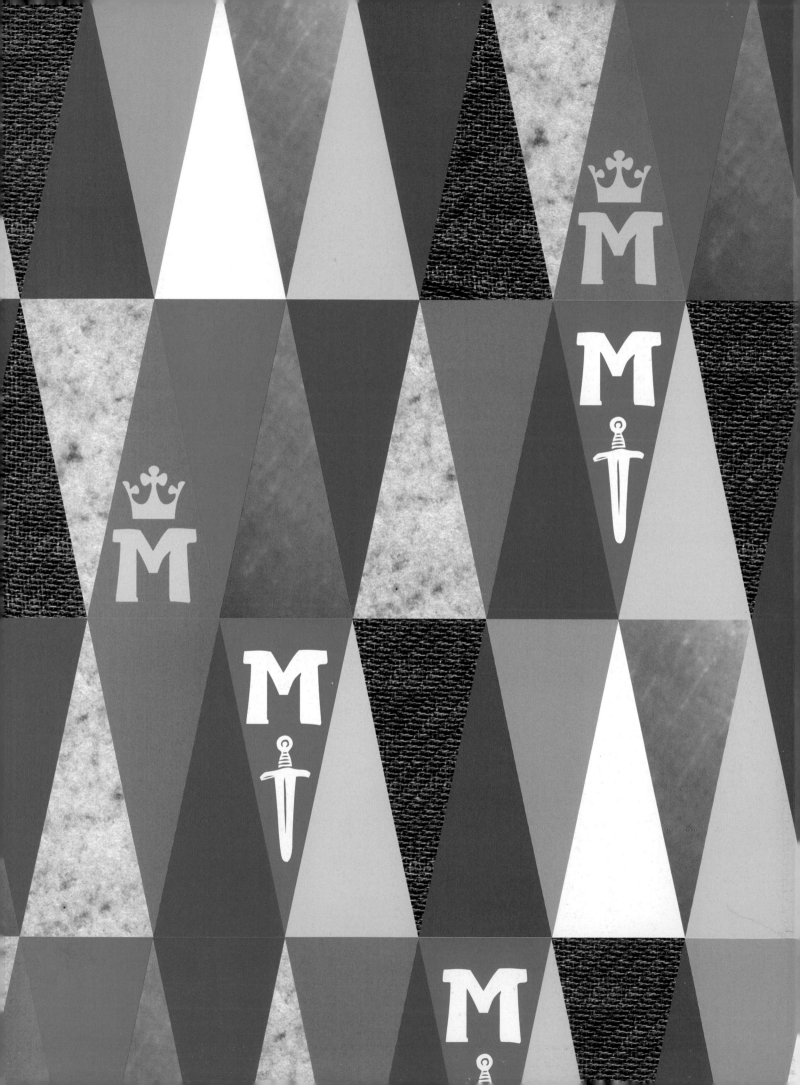